D0402950

"Behold, mortals, a beauty that will never fade."

THE SPIDERWICK CHRONICLES

THE IRONWOOD TREE
BOOK FOUR OF FIVE

Tony DiTerlizzi and Holly Black

SCHOLASTIC INC.

New York   Toronto   London   Auckland   Sydney
Mexico City   New Delhi   Hong Kong   Buenos Aires

ISBN 0-439-70040-X

12 11 10 9 8 7 6 5 4 3 2   5 6 7 8 9/0

Printed in the U.S.A.   23

First Scholastic printing, September 2004

Book design by Tony DiTerlizzi and Dan Potash

For my grandmother, Melvina,
who said I should write a book just like this one
and to whom I replied that I never would
—H. B.

For Arthur Rackham,
may you continue to inspire others
as you have me
—T. D.

Table of Contents

LIST OF FULL-PAGE ILLUSTRATIONS VI

LETTER FROM HOLLY BLACK VIII

LETTER FROM THE GRACE KIDS IX

MAP OF THE SPIDERWICK ESTATE X

CHAPTER ONE: IN WHICH
THERE IS BOTH A FIGHT AND A DUEL 1

CHAPTER TWO: IN WHICH
THE GRACE TWINS ARE TRIPLETS 21

CHAPTER THREE: IN WHICH
SIMON SOLVES A RIDDLE 39

CHAPTER FOUR: IN WHICH
THE TWINS DISCOVER
A TREE UNLIKE ANY OTHER 53

CHAPTER FIVE: IN WHICH
JARED AND SIMON WAKE SLEEPING BEAUTY 71

CHAPTER SIX: IN WHICH
THE STONES SPEAK 85

CHAPTER SEVEN: IN WHICH
THERE IS AN UNEXPECTED BETRAYAL 101

ABOUT TONY DITERLIZZI AND HOLLY BLACK 110

List of Full-Page Illustrations

"Behold, mortals, a beauty
that will never fade." . . . . Frontispiece

Map of the Spiderwick estate
and surrounding areas X

"It's an abandoned quarry." XIV

"I bet he likes you." 6

"I like fencing better without
all this junk." 12

Clang of thin metal blades 15

The coach stopped him. 17

"Don't you know me?" 20

"What kind of faerie do you think it was?" 26

MALLORY?" 31

JARED FROZE. 36

EEM TO TRICK HEN TOOK PEN 38

THAT'S PRETTY FAR DOWN." 43

WHAT HAVE WE HERE? PRISONERS!" 52

BEHOLD, MORTALS, A BEAUTY
HAT WILL NEVER FADE." 60

MY LORD KORTING." 62

YOU'RE GOING TO HAVE TO FEED US." 70

THEY'RE NOT HERE, EITHER." 78

LEAN ON THE SWORD LIKE A CANE." 82

THE STONES. THE STONESSPEAK.
HEYSPEAKTOME." 84

THESTONESSPEAK." 89

OGETHER THEY LEAPED. 92

METAL DOGS BURST INTO THE ROOM. 95

WHAT HAPPENED?" 100

KILL THEM!" 106

Dear Reader,

Over the years that Tony and I have been
friends, we've shared the same childhood
fascination with faeries. We did not realize
the importance of that bond or how it might be
tested.

One day Tony and I—along with several other
authors—were doing a signing at a large bookstore.
When the signing was over, we lingered, helping
to stack books and chatting, until a clerk
approached us. He said that there had been a
letter left for us. When I inquired which one of
us, we were surprised by his answer.

"Both of you," he said.

The letter was exactly as reproduced on the
following page. Tony spent a long time just
staring at the photocopy that came with it.
Then, in a hushed voice, he wondered aloud about
the remainder of the manuscript. We hurriedly
wrote a note, tucked it back into the envelope,
and asked the clerk to deliver it to the Grace
children.

Not long after, a package arrived on my
doorstep, bound in red ribbon. A few days after
that, three children rang the bell and told me
this story.

What has happened since is hard to describe.
Tony and I have been plunged into a world we
never quite believed in. We now see that faeries
are far more than childhood stories. There is an
invisible world around us and we hope that you,
dear reader, will open your eyes to it.

HOLLY BLACK

Dear Mrs. Black and Mr. DiTerlizzi:

I know that a lot of people don't believe in faeries, but I do and I think that you do too. After I read your books, I told my brothers about you and we decided to write. We know about real faeries. In fact, we know a lot about them.

The page attached* to this one is a photocopy from an old book we found in our attic. It isn't a great copy because we had some trouble with the copier. The book tells people how to identify faeries and how to protect themselves. Can you please give this book to your publisher? If you can, please put a letter in this envelope and give it back to the store. We will find a way to send the book. The normal mail is too dangerous.

We just want people to know about this. The stuff that has happened to us could happen to anyone.

Sincerely,

Mallory, Jared, and Simon Grace

*Not included.

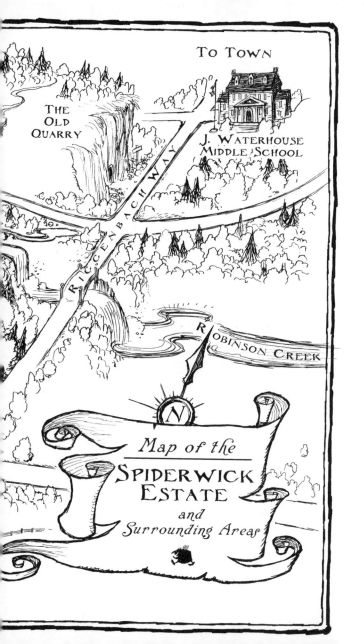

TO TOWN

THE
OLD
QUARRY

J. WATERHOUSE
MIDDLE SCHOOL

RICCENBACH WAY

ROBINSON CREEK

N

Map of the

SPIDERWICK
ESTATE
and
Surrounding Areas

"It's an abandoned quarry."

Chapter One

IN WHICH There Is Both a Fight and a Duel

The engine of the station wagon was already running. Mallory leaned against the door, her everyday sneakers grungy against the bright white of her long fencing socks. Her hair was gelled and pulled back into a ponytail so tight that it made her eyes bulge. Mrs. Grace stood on the driver's side, her hands on her hips.

"I found him!" Jared panted, running up to join them.

"Simon," their mother called. "Where were you? We looked everywhere!"

1

"The carriage house," Simon said. "Taking care of the . . . uh, a bird I found." Simon looked uncomfortable. He wasn't used to having to lie. That was mostly Jared's job.

Mallory rolled her eyes. "Too bad Mom wouldn't leave without you."

"Mallory," their mother said, shaking her head in disapproval. "All of you—get in the car. We're going to be late already, and I still have to drop something off."

As Mallory turned to put her bag in the trunk, Jared noticed that her chest looked strange. Stiff and weirdly . . . big.

"What are you wearing?" he asked, pointing.

"Shut up," she said.

He snickered. "It's just that you look like you've got—"

"Shut up!" she said again, getting into the front seat of the car while the boys climbed in the back. "It's for protection, and I have to have it on."

Jared smiled against the window and watched the woods go by. There hadn't been any faerie activity in more than two weeks — even Thimbletack had been quiet — and occasionally Jared had to remind himself that it was real. Sometimes it seemed like everything could be explained away. Even the burning water had been dismissed as simply being from a contaminated well. Until the old plumbing could be connected to a central line, they used gallons of supermarket water without Mom thinking it was strange. But there was Simon's griffin, and *that* couldn't be explained by anything but Arthur's field guide.

"Stop chewing on your ponytail," their mother said to Mallory. "What is making you

JWM

CHRIS-
THE-CAPTAIN

so jittery? Is this new team really that good?"

"I'm fine," Mallory said.

Back in New York she'd fenced in sweatpants and a team jacket chosen from a pile. There had been a guy who'd hold up his hand on your side if you had scored. But at the new school, fencers wore real uniforms and had electric rapiers wired to a scoring machine that flashed lights when someone got hit. Jared thought that was enough to make anyone jumpy.

Apparently their mother had another explanation. "It's that boy, isn't it? The one

4

you were talking to on Wednesday when I picked you up."

"What boy?" Simon asked from the back-seat, already starting to laugh.

"Be quiet," said their mother, but she answered anyway. "Chris, the fencing captain. He is the captain, isn't he?"

Their sister grunted noncommittally.

"Chris and Mallory sitting in a tree, K-I-S-S-I-N-G," Simon sang. Jared giggled, and Mallory turned toward the backseat, eyes narrowed.

"Want to lose all your baby teeth at once?"

"Don't listen to them," their mother said. "And *don't* worry. You're a smart, pretty girl and a great fencer. I bet he likes you."

"*Mom!*" Mallory groaned and sank lower in the front seat.

Their mother stopped at the library where she worked, dropped off some paperwork, and

"I bet he likes you."

eturned to the idling car, somewhat out of
breath.

"Come on! I can't be late," Mallory said,
smoothing her hair back unnecessarily. "It's my
first match!"

Their mother sighed. "We're almost there."

Jared resumed looking out the window in
time to see what looked like a deep crater.
They were driving over a stone bridge. The
school bus never went this way.

"Simon, look! What's that?"

"It's an abandoned quarry," Mallory said
impatiently. "Where people used to dig up
rocks."

"A *quarry*," Jared echoed. He remembered
something from the map they'd found in their
great-uncle Arthur's study.

"Think they found any fossils?" Simon
asked, half crawling over Jared to look out the

window. "I wonder what dinosaurs lived i
this area."

Their mother was already pulling the ca
into the school parking lot. She didn
answer.

Jared, Simon, and their mother climbed up onto the gymnasium bleachers while Mallory went to sit with her team. Already seated were a few other families and a smattering of people Jared recognized from school. A rectangular pad was spread out on the floor with lines taped on it. Mallory called it a *piste,* but Jared thought it just looked like a long, black mat. Behind it was a folding table where the scoreboard sat, its large, colored buttons making it look more like a game than something important. The director was fiddling with the wires, connecting them to a foil and testing the force needed to make the buzzer sound and the lights flash.

Mallory sat down on a metal chair at one

end of the *piste* and started unpacking her bag.
Chris squatted down to talk with Mallory. The
other team milled around the opposite end. All
the uniforms were so white, they made Jared's
eyes hurt.

Finally the director announced it was time
for the first bout. He called two fencers up and
made each of them strap a small receiver to the
back of their pants, then attached cords to their
foils. It all looked so professional. As the
fencers began, Jared tried to recall what
Mallory had said about the flashing lights, but
he couldn't.

"This is stupid. I like fencing better without
all this junk," Jared said to no one in particular.

Two matches later Jared had figured out that
the colored lights meant that the hit was good,
but the white light meant that the hit didn't
count. Only hits in the chest counted. Which

vas dumb, really, Jared had always thought.
Getting hit in the leg hurt plenty, and Jared
ad practiced with Mallory enough to know.

Finally Mallory was called to the mat.
Her opponent—a tall boy called Daniel
Something-or-Other—snickered as he put on
is mask. He obviously had no idea what was
oming.

Jared elbowed Simon as his brother put a
pretzel into his mouth. "He's going to get it."

"Ow," said Simon. "Cut it out."

Mallory's ponytail bounced as she advanced.
Her sword struck Daniel hard in the chest
before he could parry. The director raised
one hand, and the scoreboard lit up with a
point for Mallory. Jared grinned.

Their mother was craning her whole body
forward as if there were something to hear
other than the clang of thin metal blades locked

"I like fencing better without all this junk."

the pattern of attack, parry, and riposte.
niel lunged desperately, too upset to control
advance. Mallory countered, turning her
fense into an attack and scoring another
int.

Their sister beat Daniel without being
iched once. They saluted each other formally,
d the boy took off his mask, red-faced and
eathing hard. When Mallory's mask came off,
e smiled, eyes slitted with satisfaction.

On the way back to the metal chairs the
ncing captain gave Mallory a quick awkward
g. Jared couldn't see very well, but he could
ve sworn that Mallory's face flushed darker
an it had been when she stepped off the mat.

The bouts went on, with Mallory's team
ing pretty well. When it was the captain's
rn to fence, Mallory cheered loudly.
nfortunately it didn't seem to help. He was

defeated by a narrow margin. Slinking back t
his seat, he walked past her without a wor
and shrugged off her attempts to talk to him

When Mallory was called to the mat agai
Chris didn't even look up.

Jared watched from the stands an
scowled. His scowl deepened when he notice
a blond-haired girl in white fencing garb roo
ing through his sister's bag.

"Who's that?" Jared pointed.

Simon shrugged. "I dunno. She hasn
fenced yet."

Could the girl be a friend of his siste
Maybe she was just borrowing something
The furtive way the girl stopped when anyor
from the team looked her way made Jare
think she was stealing. But what would any
one want in a bag of Mallory's dirty socks an
spare foils?

Clang of thin metal blades

Jared stood up. He had to do somethin
Didn't anyone else notice what was happe
ing?

"Where are you going?" his mother asked

"Bathroom," he lied automatically, eve
though his mother would be able to see hi
walking across the gym. He wished he coul
tell her the truth, but she would have made u
some excuse for the girl. She thought the be
of everyone, except him.

Jared climbed down the bleachers an
staying close to the wall, crossed the court
where the girl was still rummaging. But
Jared approached the chairs, the coac
stopped him.

The fencing coach was wiry and shor
with patchy white stubble on his face. "Sorr
kid, you can't come over here during th
meet."

The coach stopped him.

"But that girl's trying to steal my sister
stuff!"

The coach turned. "Who?"

As Jared swung around to point her ou
though, he realized that she'd disappeared. H
fumbled for an explanation. "I don't know wh
she is. She hasn't fenced yet."

"Everybody's fenced, kid. I think you'd be
ter go back to your seat."

Jared turned back to the bleachers, emba
rassed, then thought better of it. He'd go out 1
the bathroom so that maybe his mother woul
ask fewer questions when he returned. Ju
before he walked through the blue gym door
he stopped and looked back. Now *Simon* wa
fumbling through Mallory's bag. But Simo
was wearing *his* clothes! Everyone would thin
it was him. He narrowed his eyes, wishir
what he saw made sense.

Then a horrible suspicion formed in his
ind. Glancing up into the stands, he caught
ght of his brother sitting beside his mother,
ewing on pretzels. Whatever that thing was,
wasn't Simon.

"Don't you know me?"

Chapter Two

IN WHICH the Grace Twins Are Triplets

Jared couldn't move from the doorway. He heard the clanging of swords and cheering, but the sounds seemed to come from far away. He watched in horror as the coach confronted his double. The man got red in the face, and some of the other players looked at Jared's double in shock.

"Great." Jared grimaced. There was no way he could explain this.

The coach pointed toward the large gym door, and he watched Not-Jared stalk toward it—and toward him. As Not-Jared got closer to Jared, it smirked. Jared clenched his hands into fists.

Not-Jared passed Jared without a single glance, slamming through the double doors. Jared wanted to find some way to wipe that smile off its face. He followed after it, into a hallway lined with lockers.

"Who are you?" Jared demanded. "What do you want?"

Not-Jared turned to face him, and something in its eyes made Jared go cold all over. "Don't you know me? Am I not your own self?" Its mouth curled into a sneer.

It was strange to watch it move and speak. It wasn't like watching Simon, with his tidy hair and the smear of toothpaste on his upper lip. And it wasn't quite himself either—the hair was messier, and the eyes were darker and . . .

different. It took a step toward him.

Jared took a step back, wishing for any kind of faerie protection, and then he remembered the pocketknife in his jeans. Faeries hated iron, and steel was at least part iron. He opened one of the blades. "Why don't you just leave us alone?"

THE NOT-JARED

The creature threw back its head and laughed. "You can never get away from your own self."

"Shut up! You're not me." Jared pointed the knife at his double.

23

"Put that toy away," Not-Jared said, it voice low and harsh.

"I don't know who you are, or who sen you, but bet I know what you're looking for, said Jared. "The Guide. Well, you're neve going to get it."

The creature's grin widened into somethin that still wasn't really a smile. Then suddenly i shrank back as though frightened. Jared watched in amazement as the Not-Jared's bod shrank, its dark hair paled into a sandy brown and its now blue eyes went wide with terror.

Before Jared could fully comprehend wha he was seeing, he heard a woman's voic behind him.

"What's going on here? Put that knife down.

The vice principal rushed up, grabbin Jared's wrist. The pocketknife clattered to th linoleum floor. Jared stared at the blade as th

sandy-haired boy ran off down the hall, his
sobs sounding a lot like laughter.

"I can't believe you brought your knife to
school," Simon whispered to Jared as they sat
together outside the vice principal's office.

Jared shot him a look. He had explained
several times—even once to the police—that he
was only *showing* the kid the knife, but they'd
never found the other boy to confirm the story.
Then the vice principal had asked Jared to wait
outside. Their mother had been in the vice principal's office a long time, but Jared couldn't
hear what was going on.

"What kind of faerie do you think that thing
was?" Simon asked.

"What kind of faerie do you think it was?"

Jared shrugged. "I wish we had the book so I could look it up."

"You don't remember anything that could shape-shift like that?"

"I don't know." Jared rubbed his face.

"Look, I told Mom it wasn't your fault. You'll just have to explain."

Jared gave a short laugh. "Yeah, like I can tell her what happened."

"I could say that kid stole something from Mallory's bag." When Jared didn't respond, Simon tried again. "I could pretend I did it. We could switch shirts and everything."

Jared just shook his head.

Finally their mother emerged from the vice principal's office. She looked tired.

"I'm sorry," Jared said.

He was surprised by the calm tone of her voice. "I don't want to talk about it, Jared.

Get your sister and let's just go."

Jared nodded and followed Simon, look-ing back just in time to see their mother sink down in the chair he'd vacated. What was she thinking? Why wasn't she yelling? He found himself wishing that she was mad—at least *that* he would understand. Her quiet sadness was more frightening. It was like this was all she *expected* of him.

Simon and Jared walked through the school, stopping to ask fencing team members if they'd seen Mallory. None of them had. They even stopped Chris-the-captain. He looked uncomfortable when they asked about Mallory but he shook his head. The gymnasium was empty, the only sounds the echo of their steps on the glossy wood floor. The black mat had been rolled up, and everything from the meet had been put away.

Finally a girl with long, brown hair told them she'd seen Mallory crying in the girls' bathroom.

Simon shook his head. "Mallory? Crying? But she won."

The girl shrugged. "I asked her if she was okay, but she said she was fine."

"You think that was really her?" Simon asked as they walked toward the restroom.

"You mean, was something impersonating her? Why would a faerie turn into Mallory and then cry in a girls' bathroom?"

"I don't know," said Simon. "I'd cry if I had to turn into Mallory."

Jared snorted. "So, you want to go in there and look for her?"

"I'm not going into the girls' room," Simon said. "Besides, you're already in so much trouble, there's no way you can get into more."

"I can *always* get into more trouble," Jared said with a sigh. He pushed open the door. It looked surprisingly like the boys' room, except there were no urinals.

"Mallory?" he called. No answer. He peered under the stalls but didn't see any feet. He pushed open one of the doors gingerly. Even though there was no one in there, he felt weird, jumpy and embarrassed. After a moment he darted back out into the hall.

"She's not in there?" Simon said.

"It's empty." Jared glanced past the line of lockers, hoping no one had seen him.

"Maybe she went to the office looking for us," Simon said. "I don't see her anywhere."

A feeling of dread uncoiled in the pit of Jared's stomach. After the vice principal had caught him, he hadn't really thought about anything but how much trouble he was in. But

"Mallory?"

that thing was still running around the school. He remembered how the creature had looked through Mallory's bag at the match.

"What if she went outside?" Jared said, hoping that they could still find her before it did. "She could have gone out to see if we were waiting by the car."

"We could look." Simon shrugged. Jared could tell he wasn't convinced, but they walked outside anyway.

The sky had already deepened to purples and golds. In the dimming light they walked past the track and the baseball field.

"I don't see her," Simon said.

Jared nodded. His stomach churned with nervousness. *Where is she?* he wondered.

"Hey," Simon said. "What's that?" He walked a few feet and leaned down to pick up something shining in the grass.

"Mallory's fencing medal," Jared said. "And look."

On the grass large chunks of rock formed a circle around the medal. Jared knelt down beside the largest stone. Engraved deeply in the rock was a word: TRADE.

"Stones," Simon said. "Like from the quarry."

Jared looked up, surprised. "Remember the map we found? It said dwarves live in the quarry—but I don't think dwarves can shape-shift."

"Mallory could still be inside with Mom. She could be in the office waiting for us."

Jared wanted to believe it. "Then why is her medal out here?"

"Maybe she dropped it. Maybe this is a trap." Simon started walking back toward the school. "Come on," he said. "Let's go back and see if she's with Mom."

Jared nodded numbly.

When they got back inside, they found their mother in the school entrance, talking into her cell phone. Her back was to them, and she was alone.

Although their mother was speaking softly, her voice traveled easily to where they crouched. "Yeah, I thought things were get ting better too. But, you know, Jared never admitted to what happened when we first moved here . . . and well, this is going to sound strange, but Mallory and Simon are so protective of him."

Jared froze, both dreading what she was going to say and unable to make himself do anything to stop her from continuing.

"No, no. They deny he ever did any of those things. And they're keeping something from me. I can tell by the way they stop talking when they come into a room, the way they cover for one another, especially for Jared. You should have heard Simon tonight, making up excuses for his brother pulling a knife on that little boy." Here she made a choked noise and began crying.

"I just don't know if I can handle him anymore. He is so angry, Richard. Maybe he should go and stay with you for a while."

Jared froze.

Dad. She was talking to their dad.

Simon jabbed Jared in the arm. "Come on. Mallory's not here."

Jared turned dazedly and followed his brother out the door. He could not have said how he felt at that moment—except maybe hollow.

SEEM TO TRICK HEN TOOK PEN

Chapter Three

IN WHICH Simon Solves a Riddle

What are we going to do?" Simon asked as they walked back down the hallway.

"They have her," Jared said softly. He had to blot out what he'd just heard, blot everything from his mind except Mallory. "They want to trade her for the Guide."

"But we don't have it."

"Shhh!" Jared said. He had an idea, but he didn't want to say it aloud, out in the open air. "Come on."

Jared went to his locker and got a towel

from his gym bag. He picked out a textbook—
Advanced Mathematics—that was about the same
size as the Guide and folded it in the cloth.

"What are you doing?"

"Here," he whispered, shoving the wrapped
package at Simon. He grabbed his backpack
from the locker. "Thimbletack fooled us with this
trick. Maybe we can fool whoever took Mallory."

Simon nodded once. "Okay, I think Mom
has a flashlight in the car."

They clamored over a chain-link fence at the edge
of the schoolyard and crossed the highway. The
other side of the road was overgrown with weeds.
It was hard to walk in the dark, and the flashlight
gave off only a faint narrow light.

They climbed over a large pile of rocks, some covered in slick moss, others cracked in parts. As they went, Jared couldn't stop replaying what he'd overheard. He thought about the awful things that his mother believed and the even more-awful things she was likely to believe now that he'd disappeared. No matter what he did, he wound up in deeper and deeper trouble. What if he were expelled? What if she were to send him out to live with his dad, who wouldn't want him?

"Jared, look," said Simon. They had come to the edge of the old quarry.

The rock had been mined jaggedly; chunks of stone stuck out like ledges along the nearly thirty-foot drop to the uneven valley below. Scrubby bits of grass grew along the walls from thick veins of dirt. The highway ran over the top of the cavern, elevated on a thick stone bridge.

"It's weird to mine rocks, isn't it?" Simon asked. "I mean, they're just *rocks*.

"Probably granite," he continued when Jared didn't answer. Simon wrapped his thin jacket tighter around himself.

Jared shone his flashlight along the walls, catching a streak of rust and a blush of ochre in the beam. He had no idea what kind of stone it was.

Simon shrugged. "So, uh, how are we going to get down there?"

"I don't know. Why don't you tell me, if you know so much?" Jared snapped.

"We could . . . ," Simon started, but he trailed off and Jared felt bad.

"Let's just try to climb down," said Jared, pointing. "We can jump to that ledge and then try to get to another one."

"That's pretty far down. We should get a rope or something."

"That's pretty far down."

"We don't have time," Jared said. "Here, hold the light."

Thrusting the metal cylinder into his twin's hands, Jared sat on the edge of the cliff. Without the flashlight, when he looked down, he saw only the deep darkness below. Taking a breath, he scooted off, letting himself drop to a stone shelf he could not see.

Turning, he started to stand. Light shone in his eyes, blinding him. He stumbled and fell forward.

"Are you all right?" Simon called.

Jared shaded his face and tried to keep calm. "Yeah. Come on. Your turn."

He heard the crunching of dirt above him as Simon got into position. Quickly Jared moved out of the way, feeling ahead of him for an edge he only dimly remembered. Simon landed heavily beside him with a yelp.

The flashlight tumbled from Simon's hand

nd fell into the darkness, hitting the valley
oor hard, bouncing once and then lying still,
luminating a thin path of scrub and stone.

"How could you be so dumb!" Jared felt his
mper like it was a living thing inside him, grow-
g by the minute. Only shouting seemed to keep
from overwhelming him. "Why didn't you throw

45

it down to me? How are we going to climb dow
in the dark? What if Mallory's in danger? What
she *dies* because you were such a moron?"

Simon's head came up, his eyes shining wit
tears, but Jared was as shocked as his brothe

"I didn't mean it, Simon," he said hastily.

Simon nodded, but turned his face awa
from Jared.

"I think there's another ledge there. See tha
shape?"

Simon still didn't say anything.

"I'll go first," Jared said. He took a dee
breath and dropped into the blackness. He h
the second ledge hard—it must have been fa
ther down than he'd thought. His breath wa
knocked out of him, and his hands and knee
were on fire. Slowly he pushed himse
upright. His jeans were ripped widely ove
one knee, and his arm had a cut that started t

ed sluggishly. But from there it was only a
ort hop down to the quarry floor.

"Jared?" Simon's voice came faintly from
here he was still sitting on the top ledge.

"I'm here," Jared called. "Don't move. I'll
t the light."

He crawled over to grab the flashlight and
rned it toward his brother, searching out ledges
here Simon could step or niches he could grab.
owly Simon climbed his way to the ground.
it as he waited, Jared noticed echoing sounds,
distant thrum and a pounding that seemed to
me from nowhere and everywhere at once.

Shining the flashlight around the quarry, he
w more jagged rock with faint traces of drill
es. He now wondered how they were ever
ing to get out. But before he had time to
rry about that, the light flashed on an over-
ng of rock on the wall. As the light passed

over the stone, a mottled pattern of fungi ga
off a dim bluish glow.

"Bioluminescence," Simon said.

"Huh?" Jared took a step closer.

"When something makes its own light."

By the weak glow, Jared saw that a rectang
of stone under the ledge had been carved with
pattern of intertwining grooves. Looking at t
center of the rock, he could make out the tops
letters hewn into the stone. He turned the flas
light directly on them.

SEEM TO TRICK HEN TOOK PEN

"A riddle," said Jared.

"It doesn't make any sense," said Simon.

"Who cares about that? How do we sol
it?" They didn't have time to stand around no
They were almost inside, almost to Mallory.

"You solved the one back at the house," said Simon, sitting down with his back to his brother. "You figure it out."

Jared took a deep breath. "Look, I'm really sorry about what I said before. You have to help," Jared pleaded. "Everyone knows you're smarter than I am."

Simon sighed. "I don't understand the riddle either. A hen is a girl chicken, right? And a pen would be the place where they keep chickens. I don't know about the rest."

Jared looked at the words again. He couldn't seem to concentrate. What trick could a chicken perform? Maybe they were supposed to offer eggs at the entrance? Did the Guide say anything about chickens and faeries? He wished he had the book now. . . .

"Hey, wait a minute," Simon said, turning round and kneeling up. "Give me that light."

Jared handed over the flashlight an
watched as Simon scratched out the message i
the thin dirt with his finger. Then he starte
scratching out certain letters and writing the
above in a different pattern.

MITES OPEN THREE TOCK KON

"What are you doing?" Jared sat dow
beside his twin.

"I think you have to rearrange the letters to
et the real message. Like those puzzles in the
aper that Mom is always doing." Simon
scribed a third phrase in the dust.

KNOCK THREE TIMES TO OPEN

"Wow," said Jared. He couldn't believe that
imon had figured it out. He never would have
olved it.

Simon grinned. "Easy," he said, walking up
the door and knocking three times on the
ard stone face.

Just then the ground shifted underneath
em, and both twins fell into the chasm that
ened beneath their feet.

"What have we here? Prisoners!"

Chapter Four

IN WHICH the Twins Discover a Tree Unlike Any Other

They tumbled down into a net of woven metal. Yelping and kicking, Jared tried to stand, but he couldn't seem to get a foothold. Abruptly he stopped struggling and got elbowed in the ear by his brother.

"Simon, stop! Look!"

Glowing fungi covered the walls in patches, illuminating the faces of three small men with skin as gray as stone. Their clothes were drab and sewn from rough fabrics, but their silver bracelets, crafted in the shape of serpents, were

so intricate that they seemed to slither around
the men's thin arms; their collars were woven
with golden threads beaten so fine that they
might have been cloth; and their jeweled rings
were so lovely that each of their dirty fingers
gleamed.

"What have we here? Prisoners!" said one
with a voice like gravel. "Seldom have we any
live prisoners."

"Dwarves," Jared whispered to his brother.

"They don't seem very 'hi-ho, hi-ho,'"
Simon whispered back.

The second dwarf rubbed several strands of
Jared's hair between his fingers and turned to
the one who had spoken. "Not very extraordi-
nary, are they? The black of their tresses is dull
and plain. Their skin is neither smooth nor pale
as marble. I find them ill made. We could do
far better."

Jared scowled, not sure
hat the dwarf meant.
gain, he wished for the
uide. He remem-
ered only that
warves were great
raftspeople, and the
on that hurt other
eries didn't bother
hem. His knife would
ave been useless, even if
hadn't been confiscated.

THE KORTING

"We're here for our sister,"
ared said. "We want to trade."

One of them chuckled, but Jared wasn't
ure which. With a creak another dwarf posi-
oned a silvery cage beneath the netting.

"The Korting said you would come. He is
ery eager to meet you."

"Is he like the dwarf king or something?" Simon asked.

The dwarves did not answer. One pulled on a carved handle and the net opened. Both boys fell heavily into the cage. Jared's hands and knees felt raw all over again. He slammed his fist against the metal floor.

Jared and Simon were silent as they were
wheeled through caverns with cold air and wet
walls. They could hear the sounds of hammers,
louder and more distinct now that they were
underground, and the roaring of what might
have been a great fire. Overhead in the gloom,
patches of dim phosphorescence showed the
tops of large stalactites, hanging above them like
a forest of icicles.

They passed through a grotto where bats
shrieked from above, and the floor was dark
and rank with their droppings. Jared tried to
contain a shiver. The deeper they went, the
colder the cavern became. Sometimes Jared
saw shadows shift in the gloom and heard an
erratic tapping.

As they moved through a narrow corridor,
past dripping columns, Jared breathed in the
damp, mineral scent with relief after the stink

of the bats. The next chamber seemed to be filled with dusty piles of metal objects. A golden rat with sapphire eyes darted out of a malachite goblet and watched them pass. A silver rabbit lay on its side, a winding key around its neck while a single bud of a platinum lily opened then closed, then opened again. Simon looked at the metal rat with longing.

Then they moved into a large cavern where they saw dwarves carving statues of other dwarves into the granite walls. The sudden brightness of the lantern light stung Jared's eyes, but as he passed the dwarves, he thought he saw one of the carving's arms move.

From there they moved into an enormous space where a massive tree grew under ground. The thick trunk reached up until it was lost in the shadows, branches forming canopy over them. The air was filled with trange metallic birdsong.

"That can't be a tree,"
Simon said. "There's no
un. No sun means no
photosynthesis."

Jared peered at the trunk.
It's metal," he said, realizing
hat the leaves were all of beaten silver. High in
he tree a copper bird beat its mechanical
wings and stared down with cold, jet eyes.

"The first ironwood tree," said one of the
warves. "Behold, mortals, a beauty that will
ever fade."

Jared looked up at the tree with awe,
amazed by how one metal had been forged as
ough as bark and twisted into branches while
nother was as delicate as filigree. Each silver
af was unique, veined and curled like a real
ne.

"Behold, mortals, a beauty that will never fade"

"Why do you call us mortals?" Jared asked.

"Don't you know your own tongue?" a dwarf said, and snorted. "It means one who is fated for death. What else should we call you? Your kind wither in a blink of the eye." He leaned close to the bars of the cage and winked.

Several passages led from the cavern out into corridors that were too dim for Jared to see where they led. The cage was wheeled through one—a wide, columned hallway that led into a smaller room. Sitting on a throne hewn from an enormous stalagmite was another gray-skinned man, this one with a wiry black beard. His eyes shone like green jewels. A metal dog stretched out on a deerskin rug before the throne, the dog's side rising and falling in time with a thin mechanical wheeze, just as if it were really sleeping. On its back a single key slowly turned.

"My lord Korting."

Around the throne were other dwarves, all of them silent.

"My lord Korting," said one of the dwarves. "It is as you said. They have come looking for their sister."

The Korting stood. "Mulgarath told me you would come. How fortunate you are to be here, how honored that you will see the beginning of the end of human rule."

"Whatever," Jared said. "Where's Mallory?"

The Korting scowled. "Bring her," he said, and several of the dwarves immediately shuffled off. "You would do well to watch what you say. Mulgarath will soon reign over the world, and we, his loyal servants, will be at his side. He will strip the land bare for us and then we will build a glorious new forest of ironwood trees. We will rebuild the world in silver and copper and iron."

Simon crawled to the edge of the cage.

"That doesn't make any sense. What are you going to eat? How are you going to breathe without plants to make oxygen?"

Jared smiled at Simon. Sometimes it wasn't so bad having a know-it-all for a twin brother.

The Korting's scowl deepened. "Do you deny that we dwarves are the greatest crafts-people you have ever seen? You need only to look at my hound there to see our superiority. His silver body is more lovely than any fur, he is faster, he needs no food, and he neither drools nor fawns." The Korting nudged the dog with his foot. The dog turned and stretched before resuming its wheezy sleep.

"I don't think that's what Simon was trying to say," Jared began, but he was interrupted by six dwarves entering the room, a long glass box on their shoulders.

"Mallory!" Jared stared with a sinking feeling in his stomach. The case looked like a coffin.

"What did you do to our sister?" Simon demanded. He looked pale. "She's not dead, is she?"

"Just the opposite," said the dwarf lord with a smile. "She will never die. Look more closely."

The dwarves set down the glass case on an ornately sculpted stand beside Jared and Simon's cage.

Mallory's hair had been arranged and hung in one long braid snaking past her waxy, pale face. A circlet of metal leaves rested above her forehead. Her lips and cheeks were rouged as red as a doll's, yet her hands held the hilt of a silvery blade.

She had been dressed in a white gown of frothy lace. Her eyes were closed, and Jared was almost afraid that if she opened them, they would be made of glass.

"What did they do to her?" said Simon. "It doesn't seem like Mallory at all."

"Her beauty and youth will never fade," said the Korting. "Out of this case she would be doomed to age, death, and decay—the curse of all mortals."

"I think Mallory would rather be doomed," said Jared.

The dwarf lord snorted. "Suit yourself. What have you to give me for her?"

Jared reached into his backpack and brought out the towel-wrapped book. "Arthur Spiderwick's field guide." He felt a winge of guilt at the lie but ruthlessly quashed it.

The Korting rubbed his hands together. "Excellent. Just as was anticipated. Let's have the book."

"You'll give my sister back to me?"

"She'll be yours."

Jared held out the fake field guide, and one of the dwarves snatched it through the bars. The dwarf lord did not even bother to look at it.

"Take this fine cage to the treasure room, and put the glass case beside it!"

"What?" Jared said. "But you wanted to trade!'"

"We *have* traded," the Korting said with a sneer. "You bargained for your sister, but you never bargained for your freedom."

"No! You can't!" Jared banged his hands on the bars, but it did not keep the dwarves from pushing their moving prison out into a dark corridor. He couldn't look at Simon. After all his yelling at his brother, it was he who was the stupid one, he who hadn't been clever enough. He felt tired and worn-out, small and pathetic. He was just a kid. How was he supposed to find a way out of this?

"You're going to have to feed us."

Chapter Five

IN WHICH Jared and Simon Wake Sleeping Beauty

Jared barely noticed the path they took to the treasure room. He shut his eyes against the burn of tears.

"Here we are," said the dwarf who had brought them. His beard was white, and there was a ring of keys at his hip. He turned to the group carrying the glass box that held Mallory. "Just set that down right there."

The treasure chamber was lit with a single lantern, but the heaps of shining gold reflected the light, so it was not as dim as it might have been. A silver peacock with a lapis-and-coral-studded tail pecked at a copper mouse sitting atop a vase in a way that suggested more boredom than malice.

The white-bearded dwarf peered at them while the others trooped out. He grinned at them fondly. "I'll just see if I can find something for you boys to play with. Perhaps gob stones. They even stand up and hurl themselves."

"I'm hungry," Simon said. "We're no mechanical. If you're going to keep us here you're going to have to feed us."

The dwarf squinted. "True enough. I'll bring you a mash of spiders and turnips. That will fix you right up."

"How are you going to give it to us?" Jared asked suddenly. "There's no door."

"Oh, there's a door all right," said the dwarf "I made that cage myself. Sturdy, isn't it?"

"Yeah," said Jared. "Real sturdy." He rolled his eyes. Wasn't it bad enough that they had gotten tricked and were stuck in a *cage*? Did the dwarf really have to rub it in?

"See, the lock is inside this bar." The dwarf tapped one of the bars lightly with his finger. "I had to make the gears really tiny—had to work with a hammer the size of a pin.

If you look, you can see the seam of the door
See? Right there."

"Can you open it?" Simon asked. Jared
looked at him with surprise. Had Simon been
planning the whole time, while Jared had been
busy just being upset?

"You want to see it in action?" asked the
dwarf.

"Yeah," Jared said, not quite believing that
they were going to get this lucky.

"Well, okay, boys. Now step back for a
moment. There. Just once, and then I better
get your food. What a treat to finally get to use
all of these things."

Jared smiled encouragingly. The dwarf
took the key ring from his belt and selected a
tiny key. It was the size and shape of a whistle
with a complicated pattern of ridges on it. He
inserted it into one of the bars, although Jared

ouldn't see the hole from
heir side of the cage. With a
wist of the dwarf's wrist, clicks,
lunks, whirrs, and whizzing
noises came from the whole rail.

"There." The dwarf pulled on the
par, and a front section of the cage swung open
on hidden hinges. But just as the boys were
moving forward, the dwarf quickly shut it.
"Wouldn't have been as much fun if you hadn't
at least tried to escape," he chuckled, moving to
hook the key ring back on his belt.

Jared darted his hand out and grabbed for
the key ring at the same time. The keys clattered to the floor.

Simon scooped them up before the dwarf
could.

"Hey! No fair!" said the dwarf. "Give those
back!"

Simon shook his head.

"But you have to. You're prisoners. You can't have the keys."

"We're not giving them back," Jared said.

The dwarf looked panicked. He walked to the edge of the hall and yelled, "Quick — someone! Send guards! The prisoners are escaping!" When no one came, he fixed Jared and Simon with a glare. "You'd better stay right there," he said, and darted out into the hall, still calling for guards.

Simon fitted the key into the door, and they jumped out of the cage. "Hurry, they're coming!"

"We have to get Mallory!" Jared gestured to her case.

"There's no time," said Simon. "We'll come back."

"Wait," Jared said. "Let's hide here! They'll think we ran away."

Simon looked panicked. "Where?"

"On top of the cage!" Jared pointed to the
lid silver lid of the cage. He scrambled on top
f a nearby pile of loot and used it to climb up.
Come on!"

Simon climbed halfway, and Jared hauled
im onto the top. They had just enough time to
irl up tightly before dwarves burst into the
oom.

"They're not here, either," one dwarf said.
Not in the hallway, not in any of the nearby
ooms."

Jared smirked against the cool metal.

"Wind up the dogs. They'll find them."

"Dogs?" Simon mouthed to Jared as the
warves shuffled out of the room.

"What's the matter?" Jared smiled, giddy at
he success of their plan. "You love dogs."

Simon rolled his eyes and dropped to the

"They're not here, either."

or, kicking a candelabrum and scattering a
w pieces of hematite. He picked up one and
cked it in his pocket.

"Stop making so much noise," Jared said,
ying to climb down carefully and nearly top-
ing a copper rosebush.

They knelt beside the glass case, and Jared
latched it. There was a hiss as the lid lifted,
though some invisible gas was escaping.
side, Mallory was motionless.

"Mallory," Jared said. "Get up." He pulled
her arm, but it was limp and flopped back
to her chest when he let go.

"You don't think someone needs to kiss
r, do you?" Simon asked. "Like Snow
hite?"

"That's gross." Jared couldn't remember
ything about kissing in the field guide, but he
uldn't remember anything about glass coffins,

either. He leaned in and gave her a quick pec
on the cheek. There was no response.

"We have to do something," Simon sai
"We don't have much time."

Jared grabbed a lock of Mallory's hair an
tugged hard. She twitched slightly and ha
opened her eyes. Jared sighed with relief.

"Getoffme," she muttered, and tried to tur
on her side.

"Help me get her up," Jared said, movir
the sword off her and onto the floor.

He pulled her body a little ways up befor
she slipped back into the case.

"Come on, Mal," Jared said into her ear. *"Up*

Simon slapped her cheek. She twitche
again, opening her eyes groggily.

"Wha—," she managed.

"You have to get out of there," said Simo
"Stand up."

"Lean on the sword like a cane," Jared suggested.

With her brothers' help Mallory managed to get on her feet and stagger out into the hallway. It was empty.

"Lean on the sword like a cane."

J. WATERHOUSE MIDDLE SCHOOL

DATE: __October 11__

STUDENT NAME: __Grace, Jared__

SEX: __M__   GRADE: __4__   AGE: __9__   SSN: __134-00-2067__

STUDENT LIVES WITH: __x__ Mother ___Father ___Both ___Other

__Jared Grace__ HAS BEEN SUSPENDED FROM J. WATERHOUSE MIDDLE SCHOOL FOR A PERIOD OF ___10___ DAYS.

DURING THIS TIME, THE STUDENT IS BANNED FROM CAMPUS AND ALL SCHOOL FUNCTIONS. THIS IS THE STUDENT'S __first__ SUSPENSION AND IS FOR THE FOLLOWING REASONS: On October the eleventh, Jared Grace was seen in the hallway during an athletic event, threatening another child with a knife. In accordance with our policy, any student who is found on school premises, at school-sponsored or school-related events, in possession of a dangerous weapon (see chapter 550 for what constitutes a dangerous weapon under the school guidelines) or controlled substance may be subject to expulsion from the school or school district.

WE REGRET THAT IT IS NECESSARY TO TAKE THIS DISCIPLINARY ACTION. IF YOU DESIRE FURTHER INFORMATION ON THIS MATTER, YOU MAY CONTACT ME DIRECTLY AT THE SCHOOL.

GRADED SCHOOLWORK MISSED BY A STUDENT ON AN OUT-OF-SCHOOL SUSPENSION CANNOT BE MADE UP.

WE ARE HOPEFUL OUR COORDINATED EFFORTS WILL LEAD TO A BETTER UNDERSTANDING AND SOLUTION TO THE PROBLEM.

COMMENTS:
Due to previous disciplinary problems in the classroom here and at his previous school as well as the serious nature of this incident, expulsion is recommended. A hearing before the school board will be scheduled. You and your son are encouraged to attend and present any information you feel will be material to a decision on this matter.

THE ABOVE NAMED STUDENT HAS BEEN AFFORDED DUE PROCESS AND ALL SUSPENSION/EXPULSION PROCEDURES HAVE BEEN FOLLOWED AS DIRECTED BY STATE LAW.

PRINCIPAL'S SIGNATURE_____

Carbon copy of Jared Grace's expulsion letter.

"For once," Simon said, "things are actually
ing our way."

Just then they heard the distant sound of
llow, metallic barking.

"The stones. The stones speak. They speak to me."

Chapter Six

IN WHICH the Stones Speak

Jared and Simon ran, half dragging Mallory, through a series of hallways and narrow, dim rooms. Once, they passed through an overhang high above a central cavity where the Korting oversaw dwarves laboring to stack weapons onto carts. The barking, at first far off, became closer and more frenzied. They continued on, through chamber after chamber, tucking behind stalagmites when they heard dwarves nearby, and then creeping on.

Jared stopped in a cavern with pools where white, sightless fish darted. Tiny rocks were

THE KNOCKER

balanced atop the poin
of all the stalagmite
and the sound o
water drople
echoed throug
the space, alon
with a strang
tapping rhythn
"Where are we?

"I'm not sure
Simon said.
would have remem
bered those fish, but
don't. I don't think we can
this way when they brought us in."

"Where are we?" Mallory moaned, swayin
slightly as she stood.

"We can't go back," Jared said nervousl
"We have to keep going."

A small, pale figure jumped out from the shadows. It had huge, luminous eyes that shone in the gloom. On its forehead, two long whiskers quivered.

"Wha—what's that?" Simon whispered.

The creature tapped on the wall with one long, multijointed finger, then pressed a large ear against the stone. Jared noticed that the creature's nails were cracked and broken.

"Thestones. Thestonesspeak. Theyspeaktome." It had a small, whispery voice, and Jared strained to pick out individual words. The creature tapped again. The sound was like some demented Morse code.

"Hey," Jared said. "Um, do you know the way out of here?"

"Shhhhh." It closed its eyes and nodded its head in time with something Jared couldn't hear. Then it leaped into Jared's arms, wrapping

a strong hand around his neck. Jared stumbled backward.

"*Yes! Yes! Thestonessaytocrawlthroughthere.*" It pointed into the darkness, past the pools of white fish.

"Um, great. Thanks." Jared tried to peel the creature off. Finally it unlatched, scrambled to the wall, and began tapping again.

"What is that?" Simon whispered to Jared. "A really weird dwarf?"

"A nodder or a banger, I think," Jared whispered back. "They live in mines and warn miners of collapses and stuff."

Simon made a face. "Are they all insane? It's worse than that phooka."

"*Foryou,JaredGrace.*" The creature pressed a smooth, cold stone into Jared's hand. "*Thestonewantstotravelwithyou.*"

"Uh, thanks," Jared said. "We have to go

"The stones speak."

now." He moved toward the dark place that
the nodder-banger-thing had indicated. As
Jared got closer, he thought he could make out
a crevice.

"Wait. How did you know Jared's name?"
Mallory asked, moving slowly behind her
brothers.

Jared turned back, suddenly confused.
"Yeah, how *did* you know my name?" he
demanded.

The creature rapped on the cave wall again,
an uneven series of taps. *"Thestonestellme.
Thestonesknowall."*

"Riiiight." Jared continued on. The creature had actually pointed them toward a small
opening in the wall of the cave. They had
overlooked it before. The hole was low to the
ground and very dark. Jared got on his hands
and knees and started to crawl. The cave

loor was moist, and sometimes he thought he could hear a slither or a rustle just ahead of him. His brother and sister shuffled along behind. Once or twice he heard one of them gasp, but he didn't slow his pace. He could still hear the barking of the dogs echoing through the caverns.

They emerged in the hall of the ironwood tree.

"I think it's that way," Jared said, pointing to one of the hallways.

They ran down the path until they came to a long fissure, almost as wide as Jared was tall. He looked down into the darkness. It was as black as if the crack went on forever.

"We have to jump!" Simon said. "Come on!"

"What?" said Mallory.

The barking was close behind them. Jared

Together they leaped.

saw red eyes in the gloom. Simon stepped back, then sprung across, landing hard.

"You have to!" Jared said, and grabbed hold of his sister's hand. Together they leaped. Mallory stumbled when her foot hit the rock on the other side, but she fell safely onto the cave floor. They sprinted off, hoping the dogs could not jump as far as they had.

But this passage circled around, and they found themselves back in the central hall, massive branches hanging above them, metal birds twittering.

"Where are we going?" Mallory whined as she leaned on the sword.

"I don't know," Jared said, catching his breath. "I don't know! I don't know!"

"I think maybe that way," Simon offered.

"We already went that way, and we wound up here!" The barking of the dogs was so close that Jared expected them to burst into the room at any moment.

"How can you not know where to go?" Mallory demanded. "Do you remember how you got in here?"

"I'm trying! It was dark, and we were in a cage! What do you want me to do?" Jared kicked the base of the tree as if to emphasize his point.

The leaves quivered, clanging together like a thousand chimes. The sound was deafening. One of the copper birds fell to the ground, its wings still twitching and its beak opening and closing soundlessly.

"Oh, crap," said Mallory.

Metal dogs burst into the room from several corridors, their sleek, jointed bodies effortlessly covering the distance between the entrance and the siblings. Their garnet eyes blazed.

"Climb!" Jared yelled, hooking his foot on

Metal dogs burst into the room.

the lowest branch and reaching back for his sister's hand. Simon clamored up the rough iron bark. Mallory lifted herself dazedly.

"Come on, Mallory!" Simon pleaded.

She swung her leg onto a branch just as a dog lunged. Its teeth caught hold of the end of her white dress and ripped it. The other dogs swarmed close, tearing the cloth.

Jared threw the stone that he'd been clutching in one hand. It flew past the dog's head and rolled ineffectually against the cave wall.

One of the dogs bounded after the rock. At first Jared thought that maybe the stone was magical. Then he noticed that the dog had carried it back in its teeth, metal tail wagging like a whip.

"Simon," Jared said. "I think that dog is *playing*."

Simon looked at the dog for a moment and then started to shimmy down the tree.

"What are you doing?" Mallory demanded. "Mechanical robot dogs are not pets!"

"Don't worry," Simon called back.

Simon dropped to the ground, and the dogs stopped barking suddenly, nosing him as though deciding whether or not to bite. Simon stood very still. Watching him, Jared couldn't breathe.

"Good boys," Simon soothed, his voice shaking only slightly. "Want to fetch? Want to play a game?" He reached forward and gingerly took the stone from between the dog's metal teeth.

All the dogs bounced in the air at once, barking happily. Simon looked up at his siblings and smiled.

"You have got to be kidding me," Mallory said.

Simon threw the stone, and all five dogs bounded after it. One snatched it up in its jaw and marched back proudly, the others trailing eagerly. Simon leaned down to pet their metal heads. Their silver tongues lolled from their mouths.

Simon threw the rock three more times before Jared called down to him.

"We have to go," he said. "The dwarves are

going to find us if we wait any longer."

Simon looked disappointed. "Okay," he shouted to them. Then he took the stone and hurled it as hard as he could into the other room. The dogs thundered after it. "Come on!"

Jared and Mallory jumped down. All three of them ran to the small crack in the wall and squeezed inside, crawling rapidly on their hands and knees. Jared stuffed his backpack behind him, blocking the way. Already he could hear the dogs whining and scratching at the cloth.

They felt their way in the dark, but there must have been a fork in the tunnel that they'd missed earlier, because this time there was a soft, warm light at the end of the corridor.

They found themselves standing above the quarry on dewy grass. Dawn reddened the sky in the east.

"What happened?"

Chapter Seven

IN WHICH There Is an Unexpected Betrayal

Mallory looked down at herself in disgust. "I *hate* dresses. What happened? Why did I wake up in a glass box?"

Jared shook his head. "We're not really sure—I guess the dwarves grabbed you somehow. Do you remember anything?"

"I was packing up my things after the match." She shrugged. "Some kid said that you were in trouble."

"Shhh," Simon said, pointing into the quarry. "Get down."

They knelt in the grass and peered over the

edge. A horde of goblins poured out of the caves. They skittered and rolled, gnashing their teeth and barking before fanning out and sniffing the air. Behind them was a massive monster with dead branches for hair. It wore the dark, tattered remains of clothes from another time, and big, curving horns rose up from his brow.

From the cave entrance the Korting and his dwarven courtiers appeared. Behind them came more goblins, who were pulling a cart filled with shining weapons. With that last group a prisoner stumbled along ahead of them. The prisoner was the size of an adult human, a sack covering the person's head, both wrists and ankles bound with dirty cloth. Something about the person seemed familiar. The goblins pushed the prisoner out into

ne quarry, poking the figure with sharp sticks,
ur from where the monster stood.

"Who is that?" Mallory whispered, squinting.

"I can't see," said Jared. "Why would they
eed a prisoner?"

The Korting cleared his throat
ervously as a hush fell over the
rowd. "Great Lord Mulgarath,
e thank you for the honor of
lowing us to serve you."

Mulgarath stopped.
he ogre's great horned
ead loomed over the
est of the creatures as
e turned back to the
warves with a
leer.

MULGARATH

Jared swallowed hard. *Mulgarath*. The word had never meant much to him before, but now he was afraid. Even though he knew the monster couldn't see him, he felt those dark eyes sweep over the throng and wanted to duck down lower.

"Are these all the weapons I asked for?" Mulgarath's ringing tones echoed through the quarry. He pointed to the cart.

"Yes, of course," said the dwarf lord. "A show of our loyalty, our dedication to your new regime. You will find no finer blades, no better craftsmanship. I would stake my life on it!"

"Would you?" asked the ogre. He drew Jared's fake field guide from a large pocket. "And this—would you also stake your life that this is the book I asked you to obtain?"

The dwarf lord hesitated. "I . . . I did as you asked. . . ."

The ogre held up a battered book with a laugh. Jared realized it was the same laugh that the Not-Jared had made in the hallway at school.

Jared gasped and Mallory elbowed him hard.

"You have been duped, dwarf lord. No matter. I have Arthur Spiderwick's Guide," Mulgarath said. "The final thing I need to begin my reign."

The dwarf bowed low. "You are great indeed," the Korting said. "A worthy master."

"I may be a worthy master, but I am not at all sure that you make worthy servants." He

"Kill them!"

aised his hand, and his goblins stopped their
cuffling and scrabbling. "Kill them!"

It happened so fast that Jared couldn't fol-
ow it all. The goblins seemed to surge forth as
ne, some stopping to pick up the dwarf-forged
veapons, most just attacking with their claws
nd teeth. The dwarves hesitated, shouting,
nd that moment of panic and confusion was
nough for the goblins to be upon them.

The goblins bit, clawed, and slashed until
ot a single dwarf was left standing.

Jared felt sick and numb. He had never
een anything be killed before. Looking down,
e felt like he might throw up. "We have to
top them."

"There's no way we can do this alone. Look
t them all," Mallory said. Jared glanced at the
word still clutched in Mallory's hand, its fine
lade gleaming in the rising sun. It would

never be enough to take on all o
them.

"We *have* to tell Mom what's going
on," Simon said.

"She won't believe us!" Jared said
He wiped the wetness from his eyes
with his shirt sleeve and tried not to
look down at the broken bodies in the
quarry. "What if she doesn't believe
us?"

"We have to try," said Mallory.

And so, with the screams of
dwarves still echoing in their ears
the three Grace children started
toward home.

End of

BOOK FOUR

About TONY DiTERLIZZI . . .

A *New York Times* best-selling author, Ton
DiTerlizzi created the Zena Sutherlan
Award–winning *Ted*, *Jimmy Zangwow's Out-c
This-World Moon Pie Adventure*, as well a
illustrations in Tony Johnston's Alien an
Possum beginning-reader series. Most recentl
his brilliantly cinematic version of Mar
Howitt's classic *The Spider and the Fly* w
awarded a Caldecott Honor. In addition, Tony
art has graced the work of such well-know
fantasy names as J.R.R. Tolkien, Ann
McCaffrey, Peter S. Beagle, and Greg Bear a
well as Wizards of the Coast's *Magic T
Gathering*. He and his wife, Angela, reside wi
their pug, Goblin, in Amherst, Massachuset
Visit Tony on the World Wide Web
www.diterlizzi.com.

and HOLLY BLACK

An avid collector of rare folklore volumes, Holly Black spent her early years in a decaying Victorian mansion where her mother fed her a steady diet of ghost stories and books about faeries. Accordingly, her first novel, *Tithe: A Modern Faerie Tale,* is a gothic and artful glimpse at the world of Faerie. Published in the fall of 2002, it received two starred reviews and a Best Book for Young Adults citation from the American Library Association. She lives in West Long Branch, New Jersey, with her husband, Theo, and a remarkable menagerie. Visit Holly on the World Wide Web at www.blackholly.com.

Tony and Holly continue to work day and night fending off angry faeries and goblins in order to bring the Grace children's story to you.

Who has been captured?
Is the Guide gone?
Can three weary children
do it alone?

MULGARATH

Can they face an ogre
with an evil plan
to conquer the planet
and poison the land?

Or is there someone
brave, strong, and wise
who can battle a monster
and come out alive?

?

Where is our hero?
Seek Spiderwick five.

THE WRATH OF MULCARATH
BOOK FIVE OF FIVE

ACKNOWLEDGMENTS

Tony and Holly would like to thank
Steve and Dianna for their insight,
Starr for her honesty,
Josh and Lisa for their attention to detail,
Myles and Liza for sharing the journey,
Ellen and Julie for helping make this our reality,
Kevin for his tireless enthusiasm and faith in us,
and especially Angela and Theo —
there are not enough superlatives
to describe your patience
in enduring endless nights
of Spiderwick discussion.

The text type for this book is set in Cochin.
The display types are set in Nevins Hand and Rackham.
The illustrations are rendered in pen and ink.
Art director: Dan Potash
Production managers: Chava Wolin and Karene Petrille